D1244583

Welcome to the world of
Sofia and the Grammatakia

Thankyou for purchasing this book.

This book is designed to be the most effortless way for any child and parent to learn and teach Greek as a second language. Written as a fun story with engaging characters, each word is written inline in English, Greek and Greeklish, in simple sentences, and color coding. This allows preschool children, parents and educators of any or no Greek skill level to read, learn or narrate the story in Greek, English or any educative combination of the two.

The best way to learn is by doing, so you can continue the lesson by placing stickers of the salad characters around your kitchen and make your own Greek salad as you recall the names and actions of the story in Greek with your kids.

Apart from the educational advantages of bilingualism, the Greek language brings with it a deep historical memory and a cultural wealth that is central to Greek identity.

For this reason, subjects are introduced that allow parents and educators to start discussions beyond the books, exploring Greek history, culture, philosophy, geography, academia, myth, science, and religious history. In other words, the first inspiring steps towards a classical education. And I believe that is central to our broader human identity.

I hope you enjoy,

Ιωάννης Νικολακόπουλος

Published by
GRAMMATAKIA PTY. LTD.

grammatakia.com
sofiaandthegrammatakia.com

Text, characters and Illustrations copyright © 2016 by Grammatakia Pty. Ltd.

First Published 2016 as part of the 'Greek around the house' series: Book 1

The moral right of author and illustrator has been asserted
Illustrations by Gurei Studios

Original Grammatakia Concept Characters
drawn in Thessaloniki by Giorgos Vasileiades

ISBN: 978-0-646-95281-9 (hardback)

SOFIA AND ARTEMIS
Η ΣΟΦΙΑ ΚΑΙ Η ΑΡΤΕΜΙΣ

THE GREEK SALAD
Η ΧΩΡΙΑΤΙΚΗ ΣΑΛΑΤΑ

The first book of the Sofia and the Grammatakia Series 1:

GREEK AROUND THE HOUSE

Today is Sofia's name day!

Σήμερα είναι η ονομαστική γιορτή της Σοφίας!

Simera eene i onomastiki yiorti tis Sofias!

Her cousins are coming to visit.

Τα ξαδέρφια της έρχονται για επίσκεψη.

Ta xatherfia tis erhonte yia episkepsi.

Sofia wants to prepare a salad.

Η Σοφία Θέλει να ετοιμάσει μια σαλάτα.
I Sofia theli na etimasi mia salata.

The kitchen map helps her find the ingredients.

Ο χάρτης της κουζίνας την βοηθάει να βρει τα υλικά.
O hartis tis kouzinas tin voithai na vri ta ilika.

But they are playing in the Olympic Games!

Αλλά παίζουν στους Ολυμπιακούς Αγώνες!

Alla   pezoun stous Olympiakoos Agones!

The olives are jumping.

Οι ελιές πηδούν.

I elies pithoon.

The tomato is running.

Η ντομάτα τρέχει.
I domata trehi.

Stop tomato!

Σταμάτα ντομάτα!
Stamata domata!

The cucumbers are in the heptathlon.

Τα αγγούρια είναι στο Έπταθλο.
Ta aggooria eene sto Eptathlo.

Come on cucumbers!

Ελάτε αγγούρια!
Elatte aggooria!

Why is the onion crying?

Γιατί κλαίει το κρεμμύδι;
Yiati klei to kremithi?

"No-one invited me to the salad."

"Κανείς δεν με κάλεσε στην σαλάτα."
Kanis then me kalese stin salata.

"Don't cry" says the friendly feta.

"Μην κλαις" λέει η φιλική φέτα.
"Min kless" lei i filiki feta.

"The cousins love onion in salad."

Στα ξαδέρφια αρέσει το κρεμμύδι στη σαλάτα.
Sta xatherfia aressee to kremithi sti salata.

They all jump into the bowl.

Όλα πηδούν μέσα στο μπολ.

Ola pith<u>oo</u>n m<u>e</u>sa sto bol.

Add oregano, salt and olive oil!

Πρόσθεσε ρίγανη, αλάτι και ελαιόλαδο!

Pr<u>o</u>sthesse r<u>i</u>gani, al<u>a</u>ti ke ele<u>o</u>latho!

We did it!

Τα καταφέραμε!
Ta kataf<u>e</u>rame!

Who is knocking at the door?

Ποιός χτυπάει την πόρτα;

Pios   htipai   tin   porta?

Good appetite!

Καλή όρεξη!

Kali   orexi!

Artemis ate too much.

Η Άρτεμης έφαγε πάρα πολύ.
I Artemis efaye para poli.

Glossary
Γλωσσάριο

tomato	η ντομάτα	i dom<u>a</u>ta
cucumber	το αγγούρι	to agg<u>oo</u>ri
olive	η ελιά	i eli<u>a</u>
feta	η φέτα	i f<u>e</u>ta
onion	το κρεμμύδι	to krem<u>i</u>thi
olive oil	το ελαιόλαδο	to ele<u>o</u>latho
oregano	η ρίγανη	i r<u>i</u>gani
salt	το αλάτι	to al<u>a</u>ti

Greeklish and English Pronunciation Crossreference Guide

A α	άλφα	alpha	fAther
B β	βήτα	beta	Vital
Γ γ	γάμμα	gamma	Yard + Game
Δ δ	δέλτα	delta	THe
E ε	έψιλον	epsilon	Egg
Z ζ	ζήτα	zeta	Zebra
H η	ήτα	eta	Era
Θ θ	θήτα	theta	THrone
I ι	ιώτα	iota	Era
K κ	κάππα	kappa	Kitchen
Λ λ	λάμδα	lambda	Lamb
M μ	μι	mi	Mother
N ν	νι	ni	Nice
Ξ ξ	ξι	xi	taXi
O o	όμικρον	omicron	hOt
Π π	πι	pi	Peanut
P ρ	ρω	rho	Rock - rolled on the front of tongue
Σ σ ς	σίγμα	sigma	Sand
T τ	ταύ	taf	Tennis
Y υ	ύψιλον	ipsilon	Era
Φ φ	φι	fi	Fine
X χ	χι	chi	CHemist + Hair
Ψ ψ	ψι	psi	liPS
Ω ω	ωμέγα	omega	hOt